S0-ARN-991

For my grandad

ON a SMaLL ISLaND

KYLE HUGHES-ODGERS

 FREMANTLE PRESS

On a small island, in a gigantic sea, lives Ari.

Every morning, Ari collects the flotsam and jetsam from his beach.

And every afternoon, he watches the large ships pass by.

On clear days, Ari can just glimpse
a great land on the horizon.
Intriguing. Wonderful.

One day a large ship stops at Ari's island.

The captain of the large ship tells Ari marvellous stories about the great land on the horizon ...

... about its strange buildings, its inspiring and unusual visitors and its exceptional artefacts. He tells Ari they stop at the great land on the horizon every time they pass by.

Ari longs to visit such a place, to see so many remarkable things, and to have so many interesting friends.

Months pass, but no more large ships stop at Ari's island.

On a small island,
in a gigantic sea,
Ari feels alone.

Then, one morning, an object washes up on Ari's beach.
It is like nothing he has ever seen before.

And Ari has an idea.
A dazzling idea. An irresistible idea.

Ari places the object carefully on the sand.
He brings all the flotsam and jetsam he has collected.

He works and plans and
changes and rearranges.

For days and nights Ari bangs and clinks and climbs and reaches and then, at last, he sleeps.

Ari awakes to the sound of footsteps. Many footsteps.
He looks out from his beach and finds large ships anchored there. Many ships.

The captain of the large ship has returned.

'It's good to see you, Ari my friend,' he says. 'We just had to stop and visit. You have done so much work. What a marvellous place.'

'So many strange buildings, such intriguing and unusual visitors, and the most exceptional artefacts — we will stop every time we pass by.'

On a small island, in a gigantic sea, Ari no longer feels alone.
He is surrounded by remarkable things and interesting friends.
The large ships never pass by without stopping.

On a small island, in a gigantic sea, Ari feels lucky.

FREMANTLE PRESS
25 Quarry Street, Fremantle
Western Australia, 6160
www.fremantlepress.com.au

Copyright © Kyle Hughes-Odgers, 2014.

The moral rights of the creator have been asserted.

This book is copyright. Apart from any fair dealing for the purpose of private study,
research, criticism or review, as permitted under the Copyright Act,
no part may be reproduced by any process without written permission.
Enquiries should be made to the publisher.

Designed by Ally Crimp and Kyle Hughes-Odgers
Illustration medium: acrylic paint on linen
Printed by Everbest Printing Company, China

National Library of Australia
Cataloguing-in-Publication data

On a small island.
Kyle Hughes-Odgers.
1st ed.
9781925161168 (hbk)
A823.4

Fremantle Press is supported by the State Government
through the Department of Culture and the Arts.

Government of **Western Australia**
Department of **Culture and the Arts**

lotterywest
supported

Kyle Hughes-Odgers is an Australian artist. He has held
exhibitions and created public art across the globe.
www.kylehughesodgers.com